Learning to Read, Step by Step!

Ready to Read Preschool–Kindergarten
• big type and easy words • rhyme and rhythm • picture clues
For children who know the alphabet and are eager to begin reading.

Reading with Help Preschool–Grade 1
• basic vocabulary • short sentences • simple stories
For children who recognize familiar words and sound out new words with help.

Reading on Your Own Grades 1–3
• engaging characters • easy-to-follow plots • popular topics
For children who are ready to read on their own.

Reading Paragraphs Grades 2–3
• challenging vocabulary • short paragraphs • exciting stories
For newly independent readers who read simple sentences with confidence.

Ready for Chapters Grades 2–4
• chapters • longer paragraphs • full-color art
For children who want to take the plunge into chapter books but still like colorful pictures.

STEP INTO READING® is designed to give every child a successful reading experience. The grade levels are only guides. Children can progress through the steps at their own speed, developing confidence in their reading, no matter what their grade.

Remember, a lifetime love of reading starts with a single step!

For Benjamin Levaton
—C.G.

For K.C.
—B.S.

Text copyright © 2002 by Charles Ghigna. Illustrations copyright © 2002 by Bob Staake.
All rights reserved under International and Pan-American Copyright Conventions.
Published in the United States by Random House Children's Books, a division of Random House,
Inc., New York, and simultaneously in Canada by Random House of Canada Limited, Toronto.

www.stepintoreading.com

Educators and librarians, for a variety of teaching tools, visit us at
www.randomhouse.com/teachers

Library of Congress Cataloging-in-Publication Data
Ghigna, Charles.
One hundred shoes : a math reader / by Charles Ghigna ; illustrated by Bob Staake.
    p.   cm. — (Step into reading. A step 2 book)
SUMMARY: Considers what kind of shoes a centipede might wear and how he might shop
for them.
ISBN 0-375-82178-3 (trade) — ISBN 0-375-92178-8 (lib. bdg.)
[1. Centipedes—Fiction. 2. Shoes—Fiction.]
I. Staake, Bob, 1957– , ill. II. Title. III. Series: Step into reading. Step 2 book.
PZ7.G3396235 On 2003 [E]—dc21 2002151225

Printed in the United States of America   22 21 20 19 18 17 16 15 14 13

STEP INTO READING, RANDOM HOUSE, and the Random House colophon are registered trademarks
of Random House, Inc.

One Hundred Shoes

A Math Reader

by Charles Ghigna
illustrated by Bob Staake

Random House 🏠 New York

Centipede, Centipede,
how do you choose?

Where do you shop
for one hundred shoes?

One hundred shoes
for one hundred feet.

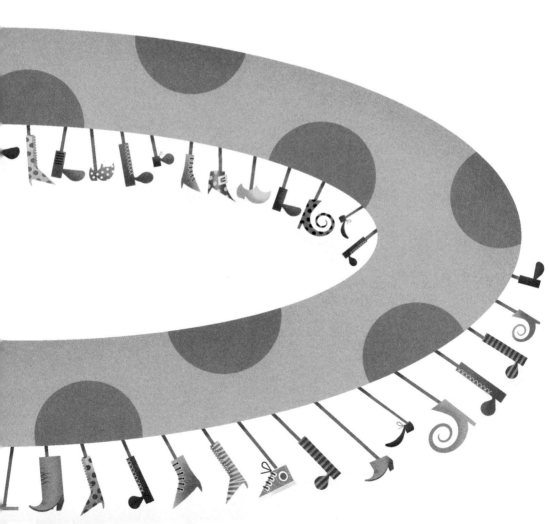

Shoes for the garden.

Shoes for the street.

Where do you buy them,
so tiny and fine?
Do you go shopping
on Web sites online?

Do you buy shoes
in stores at the mall?

Do they have sizes
smaller than small?

Shoes come in pairs.

Pairs are so nifty.

Two shoes in each pair,
so you will need fifty.

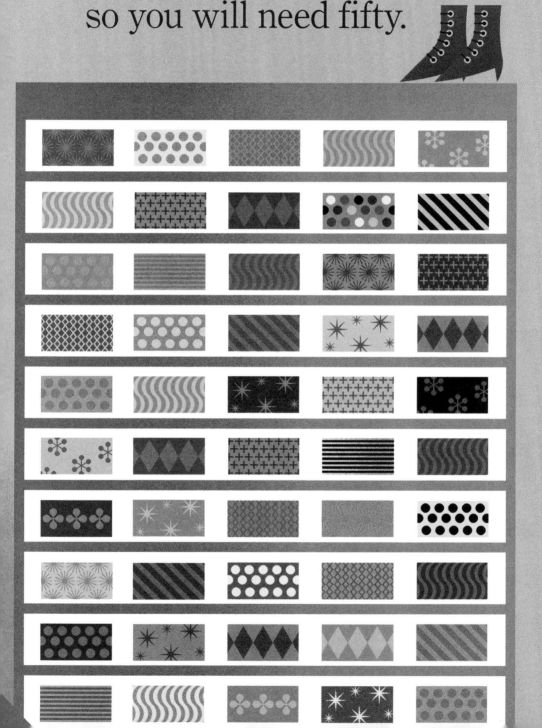

Or do you buy sets?

Five sets of twenty?

Ten sets of ten?

I hope they have plenty!

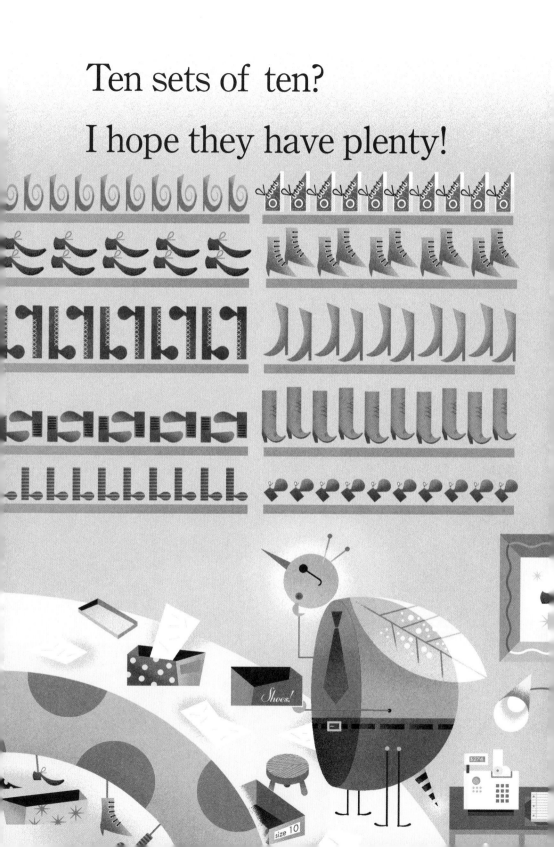

Do you wear slippers?

Do you wear clogs?

Do you wear sneakers
to climb over logs?

Do you like sandals?

Do you like boots?

Do you like loafers
to wear with your suits?

How do you tie
your shoelaces tight?

How do you tell your
left from your right?

Centipede, Centipede,
where do you keep
one hundred shoes
when you go to sleep?

Centipede, Centipede,
I think I know…

why you walk barefoot

wherever you go!

The End